To My Beautiful
Granddaughter, Alex

Christmas, 2007

From Grandma Stern

The Cat
in the
Candle Factory

Written by Barbara L. Johns

Illustrated by Carolyn R. Stich

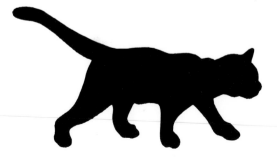

www.steepleridgepublications.com

Library of Congress Control Number: 2005901304

ISBN-10: 0-9762862-0-3
ISBN-13: 978-0-9762862-0-2

First edition published by Steeple Ridge Publications, 2005

Typesetting by KayMac Designs, Oxford, Michigan

Manufactured in the United States of America

To Geoffrey, Jeremy, and Courtney,
who loved the Candle Factory...
and the cat!

B.J.

It wasn't easy being the only cat at the Clark County Candle Factory.

Midnight was exhausted. It had taken half the night to chase all the mice away from the fat blocks of sweet wax stacked in the basement. She didn't really blame the mice. The wax was warm and wonderful and smelled like vanilla wafers. But they chewed far too much of it, and if there wasn't enough wax, Grady couldn't make candles.

Maybe there was time for a quick nap. Midnight jumped into the display window that looked over Main Street in Davisburg. She nestled into her favorite piece of old velvet and raised one sleepy eye to see if anyone was up and about. The streetlights were still gleaming, but the pale pink sky told her it was almost morning. Every front porch had a newspaper and Mr. Cobbins was opening up his coffee shop across the street. It seemed that she had just

closed...

her...

sleepy...

eyes...

when

BRIIIIIIIIIIIIINNNNNNNNNNNNNNG ! The front door scraped open and the brass bells announced that Grady was early.

"Wake up, Midnight!" shouted Grady. "We need 85 candles for Miss Emily's birthday party this afternoon! And the machine's been acting very peculiar lately."

Grady didn't even stop to scratch her ears. He rushed into the factory and stared at his marvelous candle-making machine.

Midnight was just a kitten when she helped Grady design the machine. Grady's candle business was booming and the garage was overflowing with orders, wax, and shipping boxes. After he bought the old brick building in the village, he spent hours trying to imagine a plan for a candle machine. It was a good thing she spilled ink in just the right place on his drawings or he would never have figured out how to build it!

She had ridden along in Grady's old rusty pickup truck and helped him poke around the flea market for parts. Being a cat, Midnight explored places where Grady couldn't fit, and that's how she found a wooden box of old silver roller skates. And it was Midnight who discovered the bicycle chains that would make the machine move.

She sat on the wooden boards as Grady worked and watched in admiration as he molded a big square of tin into a huge pot for melted wax. Soon a strange and wonderful contraption began to take shape inside Grady's factory.

By the time they finished hammering and tinkering, Midnight thought the tall, skinny machine fit perfectly inside the building. Like a miniature roller coaster, the track climbed from the front door up to the ceiling, stretched back to the window near the backyard, then dropped down to the floor. It was two stories tall and so long that Grady had to cut a hole in the floor to let the track run into the basement. When Grady and Midnight finished, they had linked together 176 used bicycle chains, 340 roller skate wheels, and 730 wooden boards!

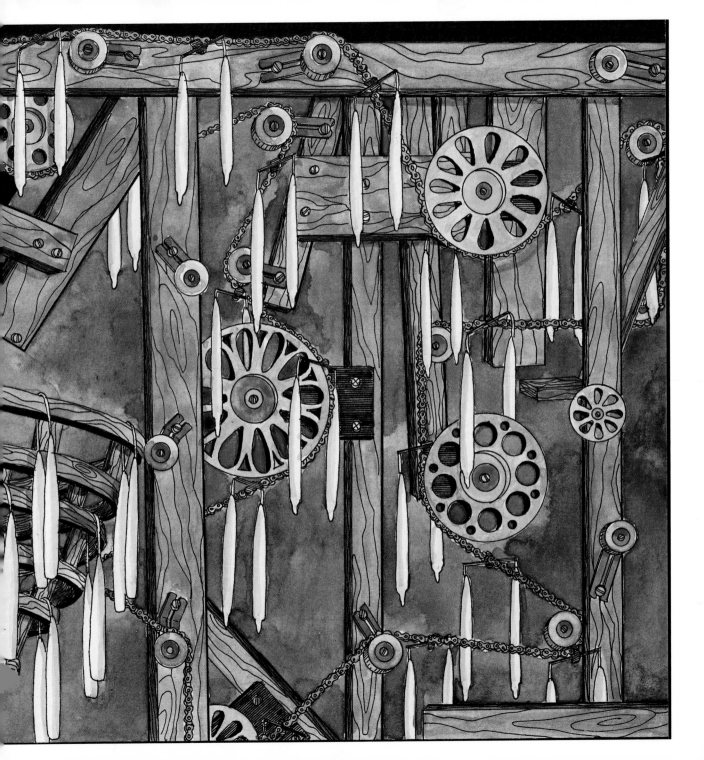

Grady's machine not only made splendid candles, but it also put on a spectacular show. People came from all over Clark County to watch the candles travel up and down, to and fro, back and forth. Every ten seconds, two white wicks plunged into hot liquid wax. When they popped back up again, the thick warm liquid had covered the wicks and rolled to the bottom of the candle with a

plop...

ploppity...

plop...

and then it would stop.

Round and round the candles went, growing fatter and fatter with every dip. They dangled and danced and sparkled under the factory's high ceiling.

For birthdays they made tiny candles, just the right size for a cake. For parties, they made tall candles to light up a dining room. In summer they made candles for decks and patios to chase away bugs. There were Christmas and Hanukkah candles, candles for the altar at church, and lovely white candles for weddings. Mario's Italian Restaurant on Baker Street used candles from the factory to make their dinner tables romantic. No wonder people came from all over to buy candles from Grady.

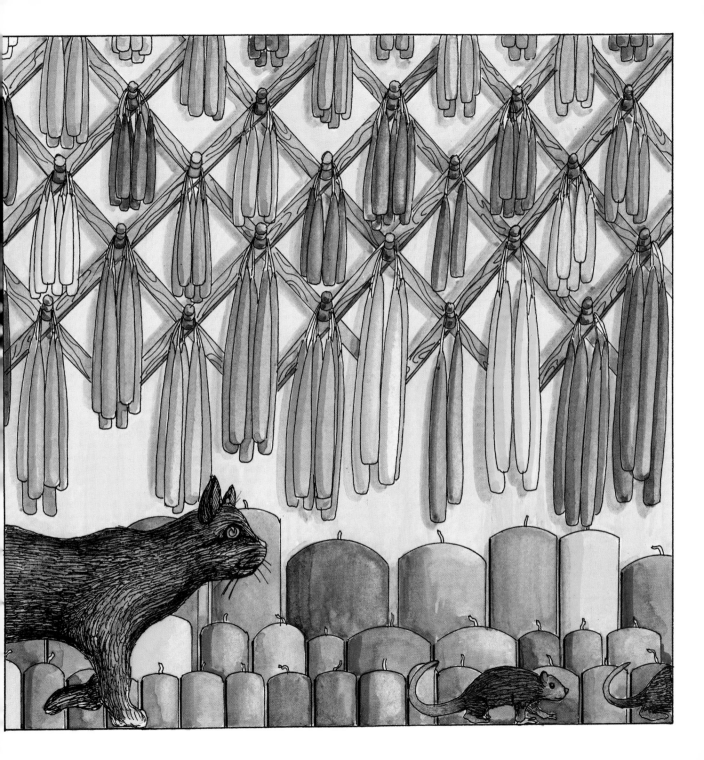

Now besides chasing mice from the basement, Midnight was also in charge of checking the machine's moving parts. She had to clamber to the tiptop of the machine — lickety split — and signal Grady if one of the chains was heading off track. While the machine hummed along, Midnight walked for hours to check that every link was strong and secure. She watched the liquid wax in the pot and added extra blocks if they were needed. With Midnight's help, Grady made repairs and his marvelous machine of recycled parts turned out splendid candles day after day.

But this morning was different. Midnight was tired from chasing mice all night. From the top of the machine she counted at least twelve rusty wheels that had to be polished and oiled before they could roll on. Eleven links in the chain were loose, and the wax pot had a nasty leak. It was past lunchtime before the machine started, and Midnight's nap was *way* overdue. She decided to take a shortcut from the top of the machine down to her velvet bed, but her sleepy eyes had trouble seeing the path.

"ME-OWWWWWWWWWWWWWW!"

Midnight's tail hit the hot wax as she tumbled off the machine.

"Oh Midnight, what happened?" Grady rushed to pick her up. "Your tail is orange!"

The next two hours went by in a blur as Grady rushed Midnight to the vet. Dr. Dorsey peeled off the pumpkin-colored wax and wrapped her tail to the tip with a thick soft bandage. Midnight was embarrassed and thought the bandage looked silly.

"Now Midnight, you're going to need more sleep," warned Dr. Dorsey. "It's not like you to be so careless." He turned to Grady. "Catnaps are really important for a cat, Grady. Maybe you need more help for the factory now that business is booming."

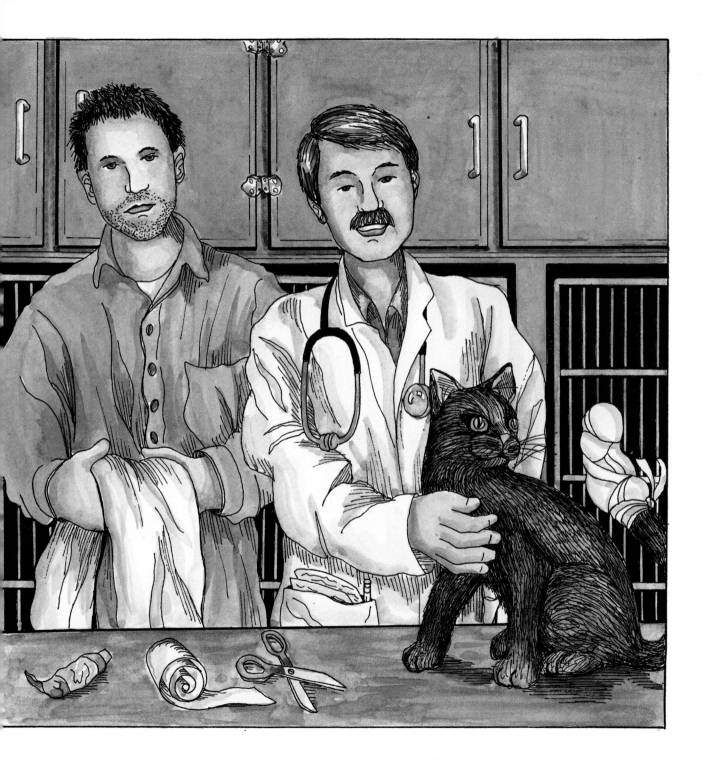

Back at the candle factory, Grady tucked a weary Midnight into her cozy bed. He had to shut off the machine and the candle orders began to pile up. The worried customers brought in special treats and catnip toys to cheer up their favorite cat. By the end of the week the hair on her tail was beginning to sprout and the bandage could come off.

But they were down to their very last candles. The mice had carried off a whole box of wax and the machine needed an adjustment way up in the rafters where Grady couldn't reach. The hardware store wanted a big order of emergency candles in case the electricity went out in town. Midnight was worried. How would she ever catch up?

The door banged open and the brass bells rang. There was Grady, bright and early, as usual.

"Don't worry, Midnight!" he said with a wink. "We have lots to do today, but I think I have the answer to our problems."

He unfolded the front of his jacket. Nestled against his flannel shirt was a tiger-striped bundle of fur. A kitten with pointy ears turned his head toward Midnight and two impish green eyes blinked in the sunlight.

"Midnight, this is Elvis," said Grady with a smile.

So the factory was fine until Christmas…

but that's another story!